The Red Door

A LOVE IN LIMESTONE NOVELLA

EMERY JACOBS

Editing: Evident Ink

Editing: Editing by C. Marie

Proofreading: Deaton Author Services

Photographer: Wander Aguiar

Cover Design: Southern Side Designs

For my readers. Thank you.

Happiness often sneaks in through a door you didn't know you left open.
~John Barrymore

DISCLAIMER:

This book is intended for readers 18 years and older due sexual situations and language. Most of the places, locations, and towns in this book are fictitious. They were created to benefit the storyline.

Preface

There's a bar on the outskirts of Limestone, Louisiana, that serves an unusual type of whiskey. Some call it magic. Others claim it's a scam, yet rumors of its mystical properties keep people coming in from far and wide.

Luck.
Wealth.
Happiness.
Health.

These wonders can be found by those who believe…and take a shot.

Ten o'clock in the morning, New Year's Day. Two down-on-their-luck strangers enter The Red Door Bar. Both are searching for a miracle. What they find when they reach the bottom of that glass will eventually change their lives forever.

Behind the Red Door

ONE

New Year's Day

Evie

THE RED DOOR glares at me.

Mocking.

Laughing.

Taunting.

I squeeze the twenty-dollar bill tightly in my left hand. It's all I have to my name, yet here I stand hoping that behind this door, I'll drink away my sadness and find health, wealth, and happiness. Then the money won't matter, at least not today. The wind picks up and I tilt my head back, taking in the dark clouds. A single snowflake hits my face, and it warms my soul just a tiny bit. No, I take that back—it does nothing for my soul. Snow during the Christmas season in Louisiana should give even the hardest of hearts joy. I roll my eyes at that thought, grab the handle, and jerk the door open. I step inside the dimly lit bar. It's small but still large enough to hold a decent-sized crowd. Only today, I'm surprised to see that it's empty. I guess most people get their *Happy New Year!* partying out of their system on New Year's Eve and spend today eating, resting, and preparing for the next twelve months. Not me. I'm not a planner. I like to wait around patiently to see what kind of shit life throws my way.

There are several high-top tables scattered throughout the room along with a few booths lining the back wall, but for some strange reason, my eyes avoid anything and everything but the lone guy sitting at the bar. His hair is dark, and it's cut short. His long-sleeved t-shirt fits snug across his muscular back and there's a denim jacket lying neatly across the stool to his right. If I were a guessing person, which I'm not, I'd say this guy is a good guy. Clean cut and decent. Someone I'd never be attracted to. I like dark and broody with tattoos. Preferably without a job or any intention of getting one. My gaze follows his right hand as he grips the small glass of amber liquid, brings it to his mouth, and throws his head back until every drop is gone. He repeats the same action immediately with his left hand, and then again with his right. And I thought I'd had a bad couple of days. This guy with his two-handed drinking has given me and my twenty dollars a reason to stay. You know, with the whole misery loves company thing and all that bullshit.

I hang back for a second or two and ogle the guy at the

bar as he repeats the same movement twice more, which brings me to wonder if he plans on walking out of this place at some point, or maybe he's hoping by the time he's done, getting home will be the least of his worries.

"Ahem." A gruff voice pulls my attention away from the guy who's on a mission to end up in the emergency room with alcohol poisoning and shifts it to the tall bearded man standing behind the bar. Has he been there the entire time? Hmm…maybe I didn't notice him because I was too intrigued by the action going on directly in front of him. The bearded guy continues to glare at me, giving me a full-body shiver—and not in a good way. It's more of a creepy, maybe I shouldn't be here way. It's New Year's Day and the bar is obviously open. I mean the door was unlocked. I glance down at my watch: it's only ten o'clock…in the morning. Okay, maybe he finds it odd that he has not one, but two people show up as soon as the doors open to morning drink.

I blow out a long sigh and give him the same glare he's giving me. "If you didn't want me here, then you shouldn't have unlocked the door," I mumble to myself.

"If you're not gonna drink, then you need to find your way out." He nods toward the door. *Happy New Year to you, too, asshole.*

"Why would I be here if not to drink? This is a bar, right?" I make my way toward the stool next to the lone patron.

The bartender scowls as he moves in front of me. Resting his hands on the bar top, he leans in a little closer than I'd like and narrows his eyes. "What'll it be?"

I glance over at my neighbor, who tosses back another

glass of the amber liquid, and then look back at the bartender. "I'll have what he's having." I motion toward the guy next to me. The bartender nods and lines up three shot glasses in front of me. He fills them quickly before grabbing the twenty dollars I already placed on the bar. I wiggle slightly on the stool, tuck a strand of hair behind my ear, and then reach for a glass. I'm normally not a shot girl, or even a whiskey girl. Hell, who am I kidding? I don't drink. Ever. I don't go to bars. Ever. And I certainly never sidle up next to some stranger hoping he'll look my way and give me a reason to want to smile.

I snag the first small glass of liquor and lift it to my mouth. The scent is not what I expected. It's spicy, minty, and warm. *Hmm…this might not be so bad.* I slowly bring it to my lips and throw it back like a pro—until it takes a wrong turn and cuts off my airway like a vise squeezing my throat. I cough once and then again, trying to regain my ability to breathe. But then something goes terribly wrong, and after a few seconds, my coughing fit grows into a tear-inducing, stomach-churning nightmare. Dammit, I'm so uncool. I turn my head away from my neighbor, slip off my stool, and cover my mouth with a napkin I swiped from the bar top. This is so embarrassing. Luckily, I somehow manage to stop the cough without any burps, sneezes, or loss of bodily fluids. Thank God. I wipe my face, crumple the napkin in my hand, and then shove it in the front pocket of my jeans. I hop back onto my stool as if nothing happened and grab my second shot. Yeah, I'm that brave. Or dumb. I toss back the minty liquid. It's warm and numbing as it races down my throat, and a small smile flickers across my face as I reach for my last shot. I place it in front of me and give myself a few seconds before I drink the last of my twenty dollars. My shitty life is somehow beginning to feel a bit better.

"Need anything else?" the gruff voice rumbles from behind the bar. I glance over at my neighbor, but he says nothing.

So my eyes flit to the bartender. "No, I'm still drinking," I say, lifting my last shooter halfway to my mouth. He growls loudly and then walks away. "He must really hate his job," I mumble, setting my shot down in front of me. I don't want to drink it yet because I'm not ready to have to leave and spend New Year's Day alone. Sitting next to a statue who doesn't speak or even look my direction is somehow better than driving around in my car by myself, trying to figure out what I'm going to do with my life.

I shift my weight a little so I'm facing my neighbor. He has a nice profile. Straight, almost perfect nose with full lips, and when he moves his mouth even slightly, a deep dimple appears on his cheek. Hmmm…I wonder if he has one on the other side. This guy is pretty handsome, but I shouldn't be looking at another guy after what I've just been through.

"So, do you come here often?" The words fall from my mouth without going through any type of filter in my brain. What the hell is wrong with me? I shake my head and fight the laughter that tries to escape. I'm such an idiot. "What I mean is: have you ever been here before today?" There, that sounds better. At least not as cheesy as *Do you come here often?* I cringe at the reality that I actually said that to a complete stranger.

My neighbor drums his fingers on the dark wood of the bar. His eyes cut in my direction, but he doesn't speak.

"Okay, I guess not. This is my first time, too." I smile

at…well, nobody because his eyes have drifted back to staring at the shelves filled with liquor that are located directly in front of him. "I wonder if what they say is true…" I hold my last shot of the minty amber liquid up between us. "If drinking this whiskey will bring me good luck." I raise the small glass to my lips and take one sip and then another, savoring every drop of the last of my drink before turning it up and taking a final gulp.

A warm tingle flows through my body, giving me a sense of boldness. Or maybe just a case of loose lips. Either way, I'm gonna sit here for a while longer, or at least until the bartender returns and makes me leave.

"I really need all the good luck I can get. This last week has been the worst." I scoot my stool a couple of inches closer to my neighbor before tilting my head slightly. "My boyfriend was sleeping with my sister. Stepsister, but she's still my sister. He decided not to renew the lease on our apartment without telling me, so now I'm homeless." My vision goes a bit fuzzy for a few seconds, so I blink once, twice to regain clarity. "Oh, and I almost forgot, he took all of my money from our joint account, so now I'm broke."

My neighbor hasn't so much as cut his eyes in my direction. But what he has done is lean forward, resting his arms on the bar, and now he's biting on a small straw that's hanging from his mouth. I'm not really sure if it's the three shots of whiskey or sitting so close to Mr. Clean Cut and Preppy chewing on a straw, but something is making me hot. I wiggle out of my oversized green coat and toss it over the chair behind me.

"Are you hot?" Again, the words fall from my mouth without any sort of filter.

I grab a napkin and begin to fan myself. I'm flushed and a little sweaty on the back of my neck. I quickly swipe my forehead and run my fingers down my hairline around my face. Luckily, no sweat there.

"Are you here because you've had a run of bad luck, or do you usually drink this early in the morning?" Shit! That was mean. What if he's an alcoholic who has really been trying to stop drinking but he fell off the wagon and I just keep reminding him? "Sorry, I didn't mean it to sound so bad. I'm really not a mean person. I usually don't drink either, so maybe that's why I can't shut up and am saying all the wrong things. It's just that…I don't know."

I shake my head as he slowly turns to face me. Wow. He's really good-looking. Bottomless brown eyes framed by thick dark lashes, a narrow nose that sits perfectly on his face, the dimple on the left accompanied by an identical one on the right. His lips are full, and his chiseled jawline is cleanly shaven. I swallow hard as he stares into my eyes. No, I take that back—as he glares at me and just happens to be focused on my eyes.

His lips flatten as his gaze narrows. "I'm dying."

TWO

Bennett

TECHNICALLY EVERYBODY'S DYING, right? I'm sure the redhead sitting next to me would beg to differ if I elaborated on what I meant when I said those two words, but damn I had to say something to shut her up because she was suffocating me. I needed air. My original plan was to slip in here this morning, have a few shots, suffer in silence, and then head back home. But for some reason the cute little chatterbox to my right decided to walk in and completely fuck up my plans. For some reason unknown to me, she felt it necessary to tell me so many things I didn't want to know. Like how her boyfriend left her for her stepsister and didn't renew their lease because he's moving out to be with said stepsister. And now she doesn't have a place to live, so technically she's homeless. Oh, and I can't forget that he also took all her money. That sums up her life in less than three seconds. I'd feel sorry for her, but something tells me she isn't the easiest person to be in a relationship with. Okay, I'm wrong for that because I don't know anything about her and it doesn't really matter what the reason is; cheating cannot be justified period. I'm sure the ex is an asshole and my new friend deserves better. I chuckle softly at the thought of calling this complete chatterbox of a stranger my friend.

Her big brown eyes get wider as her mouth opens and then closes and then opens again. I watch her closely, hoping she has somehow found herself speechless.

"First you tell me you're dying and now you're laughing?" Nope, definitely not speechless. It only took her a couple of seconds and she's back at it. "Did you forget to take your medication today?" She taps her hot pink fingernail on her chin. "Wait, I'm sorry, that sounded really mean. Let me start over. Are you taking medication that's supposed to help with mood swings or anxiety or depression?" She takes in a quick breath before sighing lightly. "Do you hear voices in your head when you're alone?" She leans in closer. "Don't be embarrassed or ashamed because there are a lot of good professionals out there who can help you. You know there's counseling, and of course medication." She reaches over and squeezes my hand, and a surge of hopefulness shoots through me. Hopeful for what? That she'll stop talking, that I'm not going to die, or that she will somehow save me from the darkness that's creeping in around me? I glance over at her. She smiles, her face lighting up, but that brightness is quickly replaced with a more serious expression.

I slip my hand from beneath hers and rest it on top of the bar. "Why would you ask me, a complete stranger, those kinds of questions?" I blow out a frustrated breath. "Do you not realize asking such personal questions about my mental health is an invasion of privacy?" I stand and drag my stool farther away from her. Maybe some distance will give her more clarity about the situation and possibly some time to think without speaking.

"I'm so sorry if I offended you. I swear I didn't mean anything by it and was only asking out of concern." She rubs her hands over her face several times before tucking a few strands of red hair behind her ears. "I just find it a bit weird that the first words you spoke to me were that you are dying but you then followed those two words with a laugh."

She's right, I am acting strange, but how do people expect me to act after the week I've had? I shift my weight slightly until my focus is back on her, because I might as well face the fact that this woman is not going to shut up.

"Can we please start over?" she asks. Her pale skin reddens, and a few splotches appear on her neck. Her dark brown eyes fill with an emotion that looks like a toss-up between regret and an apology.

"Start over?" I shake my head and let out an are-you-kidding-me chuckle. I'm sure she'll have something to say about me laughing again, but I don't give a shit. It feels good to laugh. I haven't felt like even smiling in days. I shake my head again. It's probably just the whiskey. Or maybe it's the interrogation from my chatty neighbor. At this point it doesn't even matter. I'm gonna drink and laugh until I either pass out or go home, whichever comes first.

"I'm going to ignore the laughter since we're starting over, which means you never told me you're dying."

She sits up straight, rests her elbows on top of the bar, and then crosses her legs. My gaze immediately drops to the dark denim that cover her legs. Damn, those jeans fit her perfectly, like a glove—

"My eyes are up here." She motions toward her face.

"Yeah, I was just thinking." *And checking out how hot you are, and no, I'm not embarrassed that I got caught looking.*

"About?" Does she ever let up? *Damn, woman, give a guy a break.*

"That I really need to head home. It's New Year's Day." I don't have anywhere to go, but I suddenly don't want to be here anymore. And it's not because of her; it's just I'd rather be at home suffering in silence.

"Do you have plans?"

I shrug. "Not sure."

"How can you not be sure whether or not you have plans on New Year's Day? I would think those kinds of plans would've been made in advance."

"Lately I haven't been much on making plans. But I have a sister and mother who are, and I'm sure my day is packed full of activities." It's a lie. Those two know to stay the hell away from me right now, because the last thing I want is for them to spend the entire day telling me everything's gonna be okay.

"You know, it's kind of funny."

"What is?" I ask.

"I'm not a planner either, except I don't have anyone

who schedules my day. I kind of just wait around and see if anything happens or someone calls."

"Well, it was nice meeting you," I say, mostly to be nice. After all, I am a nice guy, and I'm not really into hurting anyone's feelings.

"Was it really? Because you don't act like you enjoyed meeting me."

"Look—"

"Evie. My name's Evie."

"Look, Evie, you seem like a nice girl, like you've really got your shit together even after what happened to you with your ex." Another lie. This woman does not have her shit together, but it's not my place to make her feel worse than the asshole who left her high and dry did. Also, a part of me actually feels bad for her because no one should be treated the way she was, even if her nonstop talking is extremely irritating.

"But I talk too much."

"I was gonna say you're beautiful and if I were in a different place with my life right now, I'd ask you to have dinner with me next week." It's true. She's beautiful and sexy. Definitely my type, except for the nonstop talking. But this is not the time for me to date anyone.

My phone vibrates inside the front pocket of my jeans, and that's my cue to go. "My ride's here, so I need to head out." *Go now, walk away.* I push off my stool and stand, but I don't leave yet. My gaze hesitantly meets hers, and she smiles. I'm assuming it's at what I said, but I can't be sure with her.

"Really?" She quickly shakes her head. "Don't answer that because I know you're just being nice to me because my life is such a mess right now." Evie shoves off her bar stool, grabs her coat, and slips it on. She looks toward the floor briefly and I catch a glimpse of her expression. The little bit of happiness she was wearing earlier has disappeared, and I don't know why, but it feels like a direct punch to my gut.

I force myself to ignore her questions because I'm honestly not in any shape to dig deeper into any part of our conversation.

"Maybe I should go, too. I'm out of whiskey and money," Evie mumbles as she pulls her phone from the pocket of her coat, slides her finger over the screen, and begins typing. Once she's done doing whatever she's doing, she falls in step next to me and we head toward the exit. I catch a hint of her sweet scent and suddenly want to bury my face against her neck and breathe it in for as long as she'll let me.

"Y'all done?" The gruff sound of the bartender's voice moves through the air behind us, bringing me out of my few seconds of insanity. I glance over at the redhead, and she nods.

"Yep. See ya next time, Hal." I throw my hand up in a backward wave before we walk out the door.

You see, it's not that I'm what you would call a regular here. I've known Hal since we were teenagers. His family has owned this bar forever. He doesn't talk or ask questions. He just grunts, occasionally chews on a toothpick, and slings drinks. So, when I need to clear my head, I sidle up to the bar, order a drink, and think. No matter what time of day it is.

"I really want to ask you more questions, about your dying comment, but I won't pry because I can tell you don't want to talk about it," Evie says as she stops just outside the door of the bar. She shakes her head, and when she looks up at me, her eyes are filled with unshed tears. Fucking great. I've given her another reason to cry. "Sorry." She quickly wipes away a couple of loose tears from her face. "I just can't hear the reason why you're dying."

"I thought we weren't going to talk about my dying comment. Didn't we agree to start over?" I ask, glancing toward the road. *Where the hell is he?*

Evie shoves her hands into the pockets of her coat and shivers. "Yeah, you're right. We did. I'm sorry, I shouldn't have brought it up again." The cold air whips around us and she continues to tremble. The guy I used to be would wrap her up in my arms, pull her in close, and keep her warm. But that guy…he's gone, and if things don't change, he may not be coming back.

My brother-in-law turns into the gravel lot, stopping a few feet away from us. "That's me." I motion toward the white Ford F-150.

"Yeah, I figured." Evie glances at my brother-in-law's truck and then back at me.

"Do you have a ride home?" Of all the questions I could've asked, I just had to end it with home after she told me earlier she's homeless. *I'm such an insensitive bastard.*

"Yeah, I'm good. My friend is on her way." She blinks a couple of times, her focus never leaving me. "Good luck." She shakes her head. "I mean, crap." She fiddles with the sleeve of her coat as her eyes scan the parking lot before landing back on me. "What I meant to say is good luck with whatever's going on in your life."

"Thank you," I say as I move toward the truck. I only

make it a few steps before I stop and look back at her. "Hey, if you're still living around here next year, meet me back here on New Year's Day at the same time."

"Okay, it's a date," Evie says, smiling.

I nod. "Yeah, a date." *If I'm still alive.*

The Guy in Room 640

THREE

April

Evie

"TOUGH DAY?" I ask Regina, one of the nurses I work with here at Highland Medical Center. After the horrible beginning of this year, I managed to pull my shit together and somewhat get my life back on track. I now live alone in a small one-bedroom apartment just a few blocks away from the hospital, so I'm able to walk to work most days. If it's raining or too hot outside or if I just don't feel like the walk, I take an Uber. I'm hoping in a couple more months I'll have enough money saved to buy a car.

"Just another day in paradise." Regina's mouth remains in a straight line stretched across her face. I like to call it her neutral face, only it's really the only expression she ever wears. No smile. No frown. Nothing. Her eyes, too. No lifting and lowering of the eyebrows. Absolutely no emotion. This woman has the most non-expressive look on her face all the time. I bet she's an excellent poker player.

Tonight's my last night of seven in a row, and all of my patients from the previous nights have been discharged. There's nothing like starting over with new patients on my final night here. I shake my head at that thought, but on a positive note, I'll be taking care of the four patients Regina had today, which means I don't have to bounce around from nurse to nurse to get report. I'll get everything I need from her and then get my night started.

Regina's quick to give only what I need to know. No patient or family gossip with her, just facts. Her personality may be dry, but her attitude is nothing but professional. She finishes up with patient four, who had gallbladder surgery earlier today and gave the doctor a scare, buying himself an overnight stay. I gather up my things and head toward the nurses' station.

"Hey, Evie. I'm not done," Regina calls out from behind me. I glance down at the notes I took on each patient. Everything appears to be complete. No gaping questions on my part.

"Yeah, what did I forget?" I make it sound like it's my fault because being on Regina or anybody else's shit list is not where I want to be.

"Your last patient." She's fidgeting with the pen in her hand as I turn around and make my way back to her.

I laugh lightly because I'm hoping this is her way of making a joke. I checked the board twice and I swear I only saw four patients, but it's all good. I mean I've taken care of five, even six patients before, but lately we've been staffed so no one gets more than four, three if you're the unlucky one on admits.

"Sorry," I say hesitantly. "I didn't realize I had a number five—I assumed—I mean five is good. It'll just keep me busier so my night will move along faster." I try to force a smile, not wanting her to see my irritation that I'm probably the only nurse with five patients. My assignment isn't Regina's fault. It's whoever is in charge tonight, and I didn't even think to check the board to see who the charge nurse is. Even though I'm annoyed, I really don't care. Right now, I just need to get report on my fifth patient and get to work so I can get through this shift, go home, and relax for the next seven days.

"It's room 640."

"Wait, isn't that room like in BFE?" I ask, slightly annoyed. Regina stares at me. No, not at me—through me. Regina is staring through me. Great. I guess I've pissed her off. "I'm sorry. I just wasn't expecting five patients on my last night, and then when you tell me this patient is about a mile away from my other four…it just hit me the wrong way." A mile is probably stretching the truth a bit, but room 640 is definitely off the beaten path. "Those rooms in the back are only used if we fill up or if—"

"He has cancer. They wanted to keep him as far away from the other patients as possible."

"He has cancer?" I throw her statement back as a question because I'm confused as to why we're taking care of a cancer patient at Highland. The oncology clinic here in town likes to send patients with cancer complications to The Cancer Center of Southeastern Louisiana to keep them out of the hospitals so they won't be exposed to anything and everything that might wreak havoc on their weakened immune systems.

"Yes, lymphoma to be exact. And before you ask, the cancer hospital is on diversion."

"How many beds do they have? I mean, it seems kind of strange for them to be on diversion."

Regina looks at me with furrowed brows. "Evie, I'm ready to go home. So, do you want the report, or do you want to stand here and discuss the ins and outs of why the cancer hospital can't accommodate Mr. Stern?"

"Mr. Stern?" My mind is everywhere but here, and I have no idea why.

Regina shakes her head before blowing out an exasperated breath. "Mr. Stern is the patient in room 640. Are you feeling okay, Evie?"

I'm not sure. This unfocused person residing inside my body needs to pull her shit together. I just have to make it through tonight and then I'll have seven days to regroup before starting over again.

"Yeah, I'm fine. Just a bit tired. You know how it is, last night of seven."

"I know exactly how it is because that's where I'm at, too." I give her a shaky smile and nod before she continues. "Anyway, Mr. Stern came in around noon with dehydration from his chemo treatments. He's really fine, otherwise. We're just giving him fluids and monitoring him. He doesn't have any meds tonight, and I figure the doctor will send him home tomorrow."

After hearing the rundown on Mr. Stern, I feel a bit of relief about taking care of the guy in room 640. To be honest, initially I was terrified that he may be really sick, because chemo treatments can cause a lot of problems, but thankfully it sounds like he's not. Even though dehydration is not good, it could be a whole lot worse.

"Anything else?" I ask, not really giving her time to answer before turning to walk away.

"Oh, and 640 is on reverse isolation." Great. A full twelve hours of suiting up and stripping down.

I stop mid-step and look over my shoulder at Regina. She smiles because she knows how much fun my night's gonna be. "Yeah, okay. See ya next time." I nod as I turn away from her again, ready to get my night started.

FOUR

Bennett

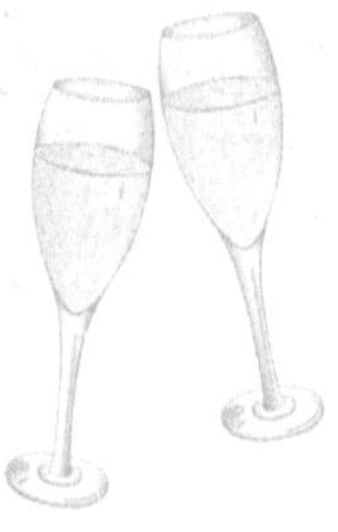

"I'M Evie and I'll be your nurse tonight." The woman's voice is soft and muffled. Her hips sway slightly as she writes her information on the whiteboard in front of me. I squeeze my eyes closed because the last thing I need to do is become infatuated with my gowned, gloved, and masked nurse. This reverse isolation is bullshit. I haven't seen one person's entire face since they locked me away in this room a few hours ago.

She turns to face me, and my heart freefalls into my stomach. Evie is tall with a slight flare at her hips. She's wearing one of those damn yellow gowns over her scrubs, but it fits snug against her body, giving me the illusion that she's not wearing two layers of clothes. Her hair is covered with an almost transparent blue cap, giving me a glimpse of a thick auburn mane hiding out underneath. But I guess what pisses me off the most is the blue mask covering almost her entire face. She takes a few steps toward me, and I raise the bed until I'm sitting up.

"Are you feeling okay?" Her deep brown eyes skim my hairless head and then quickly travel over my face, finally landing on my hospital-issued gown.

I was until you walked in the room and took my breath away. Yes, I'm pathetic, and no, I would never say those words out loud. It's just been a long time since I've been near a woman who gives off a vibe that I find attractive. Even though I can't see her face, I just know there's something about her that could easily set my insides on fire. *See, still pathetic.*

"Yeah, I'm good." I choose my words wisely because I don't want her to think I'm some kind of creep. Her eyes brighten a little and then wrinkle around the edges, and it's obvious she's smiling behind her mask.

"I'm going to assess you and then I'll leave you alone for a while," she says as she moves in closer and pulls the covers back a bit. She gently lifts my wrist with her purple glove-covered hands, looking at my IV. She gently presses against the skin around it, keeping her focus on that tiny catheter inserted into my arm. She must like what she sees because she places my arm back onto the mattress and then moves to the IV pole next to the bed. She checks the fluids and then the tubing before glancing at the pump.

"Are you having any pain?" she asks as her gaze finds its way back to mine.

"Uh, no. No pain. You know I'm not really sick, right?" I shift my weight slightly so I can see her better.

She blinks a couple of times before focusing on me again. Her eyes tell me she's not sure how to respond to my question. I have cancer, so technically I am sick, but the only reason I'm stuck in this hospital is because I somehow fooled around and let myself get dehydrated.

"You don't have to answer that question." I rub the back of my neck with my IV-free hand and then blow out a deep breath.

"Yes, I know you're not sick, Mr. Stern. Sometimes when taking chemotherapy, people get dehydrated. It's not uncommon. We wear all of this"—she motions toward her gown then her mask and cap—"to protect you from us."

"Please don't call me Mr. Stern."

She nods and cuts her eyes away from me. Dammit. I really just need to shut the hell up so she can do her job and be on her way.

But for some reason, I can't seem to stop talking. "Bennett. My name is Bennett." I smile.

"I know." The corners of her eyes wrinkle again, and I know she's smiling back. She moves near the bed and lifts her stethoscope from around her neck. "Do you mind sitting up straight so I can listen to your lungs?"

"Sure." I do as she asks, taking in deep breaths and then exhaling. Once she's done with my lungs, she moves her stethoscope around to my chest and leans in closer. I try so damn hard not to breathe in her scent, but I can't help it. She's so close. She smells good—really fucking good. Sweet, but not too sweet, just enough to recognize that it's familiar. Evie's familiar. I narrow my eyes a little to see if there is anything else I might recognize about her, and that's when I notice the four tiny freckles scattered across her nose. Freckles are not something I'd normally notice on a woman, but being so close to Evie is supercharging my senses. Or maybe it's not her at all. It's more than likely because it's been so long since I've been this close to a beautiful woman.

She slowly moves away from me and walks over to the computer mounted on the wall. "Your lungs sound clear and your heart sounds good. Also, your vital signs that were taken earlier were all normal," she tells me as her fingers glide across the keyboard.

I watch her intently as she shifts her weight from her right leg to her left. She tilts her head slightly while staring at the computer screen. Her sweet scent still lingers in the air around me, and it's driving me insane because it's too familiar. Then it hits me, and I'm taken back several months ago to my one and only stint of morning drinking at The Red Door. New Year's Day, to be exact. Red hair, porcelain skin, tight black jeans, and the scent of something sweet. *Evie.* Did she tell me she was a nurse? Hell, she told me so much that morning I'd never remember it all even if I tried.

"Are you comfortable? Do you need anything before I go?" She slowly makes her way over to my bedside, pulling me away from my memories and back to reality.

My gaze meets hers and I swallow hard. Does she know who I am? She has access to my chart, which would pretty much give her any information about me that she wanted. My mouth twitches a couple of times until I'm smiling more like an idiot and less like a guy who's in the hospital because he's not strong enough to withstand his cancer treatment without dehydrating.

Evie's eyes move over my face and stop briefly before she gives her head a subtle shake. Does something about me look familiar to her too? Granted, I had hair and maybe a little stubble on my chin the last time we met, but there's still a chance something could've triggered a memory.

"If you don't need anything else right now, then I'll be going. If you need me later, just hit the call button." She motions toward the monitor next to the bed. "I'll be back to check on you in a couple of hours." She turns away from me and heads toward the door.

"Evie." I call out to her before she reaches it. Why? I'm not sure, other than needing to know if it's her.

"Yeah?" She spins around, her gaze meeting mine.

"Do you remember me?" My heart beats a little harder as I wait for her answer.

She blinks once and then again before she nods slightly. "Yes." The corners of her eyes wrinkle again so I know she's smiling. "It's the dimples."

"Dimples?"

"Yeah, I saw the one in your right cheek first, and then when you smiled and I saw the other one, I recognized you immediately." Evie laughs softly.

"Why didn't you say anything?" I turn slightly in the bed so I'm facing her.

She shrugs. "I didn't think it was appropriate, and I didn't want to bring up memories of a day I'm sure you've already forgotten."

"I haven't forgotten that morning, or you." I'm sure I sound like a cheesy liar.

Who continues to think about someone for months after just a short encounter? Uh, hmmm…that would be me. She was beautiful that morning. A whole lot distraught, but beautiful. I even told her so.

"Yeah, okay. Well, it was good to see you again. I mean…I wish we could have seen each other again under different circumstances." She's backtracking. I'm sure this entire situation makes her uncomfortable. Evie being uncomfortable somehow comes across as adorable. I really like this side of her. Very professional, yet cute at the same time. "But anyway…" Evie shakes her head and looks toward the floor.

"It's really good to see you again too," I say in an attempt to make her feel less awkward.

She nods, her voice almost a whisper when she says, "Yeah."

"I'm sorry if me saying I haven't forgotten you makes you feel uncomfortable." I hope she doesn't think I'm coming on to her. Because let's face it—I'm lying in a hospital bed trying to get stronger so I can be ready for my next chemo treatment, and hitting on her is the last thing I need to be doing today. *And I'm not. Really, I'm not.* It's just that Evie was the last beautiful woman I met before I started my treatments. So, I believe me thinking about her from time to time is normal.

"It didn't make me feel uncomfortable. Not at all." She fidgets with the hem of her sleeve. Her eyes move around the room for a few seconds before finally landing back on me. "I'm glad I got to see you again even though the situation is not ideal." Her eyes wrinkle a little. "I really hope everything works out for you, Bennett. And don't let being in here because of dehydration get you down, because it is more common than you might think. Especially when going through chemo-therapy."

"I hope so too. The doctors say I have a really good chance of beating this." I try to sound optimistic and confident, but it's hard because no one really knows what's going to happen over the next few months.

"You should listen to your doctors because it sounds like they know what they're talking about."

"Yeah, I do have a team of great doctors."

"I need to get back to work," Evie says as she begins to move toward the door.

"Oh, yeah, sure. I guess you have other patients to take care of." I wish she could stay and talk. *Stay and talk*...I hold back a laugh because last time we were together, all I wanted was for her to stop talking.

"I'll be back in a couple of hours. If you need something sooner, just call," Evie says as she turns away from me and hurries out of the room.

You...Again

FIVE

July
‾‾‾‾‾

Bennett

THE BELL above the front door of the cleaners sounds, and it prompts me to force myself to get up from behind this desk. It's not like I'm doing anything other than just sitting here alone in this dimly lit room feeling sorry for myself. Why? Because my life has pretty much turned to shit over the past few months. Granted, I am thankful to be alive, but sometimes I lose control of my emotions and find myself wallowing in self-pity. Pathetic, I know, but right now there doesn't seem to be anything I can do to pull myself out of my current funk, and I refuse to ask for help, at least not yet.

I walk out of the office and down the long hallway, making my way to the lobby. It's kind of late in the day for customers. We had our usual after-work rush about an hour ago, and we normally lock the doors at six thirty, which is in five minutes. I push open the door that separates the back area from the lobby then turn toward the counter, and that's when I see her. *Evie.* Standing in front of a pile of clothes. My gut twists into a tight knot and my brain is telling me to turn around and get someone else to take care of her, but I don't, mostly because everybody else has left for the day. *This is what you get for letting them leave early.* The other reason I want to tuck tail and run away is because I'm not sure I know what to say to her, or how to talk to her. It's a weird feeling to have about someone I barely know. It's kind of unsettling. I mean I want to see her, talk to her, hell even ask her out, but I'm not sure I'm ready. There's no guarantee this cancer shit is gone, and until I'm confident the battle is won, I'm not about to drag anybody else into my life.

I grab the small form and a pen before turning to face her. "Are all of these items to be dry-cleaned?" I ask, trying to avoid eye contact. I'm still not sure why I don't want to look at her or let her see it's me because she took care of me in the hospital. She saw me at my worst—she knows every-thing. Why my skin is pale, why I'm so thin, and why my hair is only sparsely covering my head.

"Um…not all. This pile is press only, and this one is to be washed, and only this…" She shuffles through the items of clothing before pulling out a small black dress. "This is the only one that needs to be dry-cleaned." Her sweet smell hits me in the face, and I have to look away.

I tell myself the only reason she is having this type of effect on me is because my mind is so fucked up. I'm sad and lonely. I also am lacking female companionship, and that alone can make a man crazy and starved for attention from a beautiful woman.

"It's you." Evie's soft voice is full of recognition.

I return my focus to her and nod. "Yep. It is me." My heart picks up its pace some at the revelation that she recognizes me. Yeah, it makes me happy, but I can't let my thoughts go to a life where we can date and do normal couple things. *Damn, man, all she said is "It's you." It's not like she just confessed her undying love for you. Get a fucking grip.*

"How have you been? Bennett, right?" Her dark eyes brighten as she smiles.

Small talk—great, just what I want right here at closing time. I remember how talkative she was the first night I met her at The Red Door, but she was different in the hospital. Very professional and only spoke about medical stuff, never venturing off into anything personal. I guess now that she's somewhere other than the hospital, she's gonna revert back to being the chatterbox.

"Good. I've been good." Health-wise, the doctors say my prognosis is excellent. They caught the cancer early and treated it aggressively. Mentally, though, I'm so far from the man I used to be that it's hard to believe I was ever anything but this pathetic person who sits around feeling sorry for himself.

"I'm really glad to hear it. You look great." Her smile widens before she continues. "Your color has come back nicely, and your hair looks to be thicker and maybe a bit darker than before." Her gaze moves from my face and hair to slowly surveying the lobby.

There're so many things I hate about cancer. So. Many. Things. One being that when people see you, the first thing they do is comment on how good you look. Even when I was weak, bald, and going through chemo, people always told me I looked good. Or I looked strong. Or I looked like I was beating this terrible disease. Honestly, I would rather not hear a rundown on my appearance. I just want to talk about normal everyday stuff, like the weather or football or the new Italian restaurant that opened two blocks over.

"So, you work here?" Her eyes flit to mine, and she laughs. "I mean, I see you are working here, it's just that I've never seen you here before. It's normally Tess who helps me."

"Tess is my sister." I keep my end of the conversation short and only tell her what she needs to know. There's no sense in prolonging our time together today, because what you see is what you get: a man with cancer talking to a beautiful redhead who is always so upbeat and full of life, two things I'm not.

"Oh, I hope she's not sick." Her eyes widen when she realizes what she said. I guess bringing up the word sick around me makes her feel bad. *That's all I need is one more person to feel sorry for me.* "I mean, I hope everything is okay with her." She's backtracking, and I feel like shit that she suddenly feels like she has to walk on eggshells when she's around me.

"Tess is fine. She had to go work at the store in Matlock —the manager there is out because his wife just had a baby." Matlock is a small town about fifteen miles from here. I told Tess I didn't mind driving five minutes to this location, but I didn't want to go any farther..

"I knew Tess managed this store, but she's in charge of that one too?" Evie shifts her weight and leans against the counter.

The talkative Evie is definitely back, and I'm really not sure how to make her stop talking and leave. Or maybe the real problem here is not knowing if I do want her to leave… *Yes. No. Fuck.*

"My family owns all the City Cleaners here in Riverport, the one in Limestone, and the one Matlock. This location is the one Tess works out of."

"Hmm…so Tess is your sister. That's interesting," she says, resting her elbow on the counter.

"Yeah she is, unfortunately." I chuckle, and it startles me. Laughing is something I haven't done in a long time, and after spending less than five minutes with Evie, I forget who I am, what I'm fighting, and why I can't allow myself to become too relaxed.

"Wow. It's a small world, huh?"

"Yep. Pretty small." I begin to separate her clothes into small piles before filling out the intake information. "I just need your last name and phone number." I let my attention leave her completely and focus on my job.

"Oh, sorry, sure. Tucker, Evie Tucker, and my number is 442-6521."

I take down all her information before I begin tagging her clothes.

"Which location do you work at?" She continues with her game of twenty questions, and I've learned from the short time I've been around Evie Tucker that this is what she does. She talks nonstop and is full of inquiries.

"I don't work at any of the locations. I'm only helping out when she needs me." I'm thankful for the business my parents built, but running a dry cleaners is not something I've ever been interested in. It's why I went to college and got my engineering degree. I prefer the oilfields of Texas to the cleaning solutions and pissed-off customers here at home.

Evie smiles, and surprisingly, she doesn't ask another question. "That's really nice of you to help out. I'm sure Tess appreciates it."

I finish tagging her items and put them in a bag. "She does," I say. She better. She pulled me from an entire day of lying around the house wondering if I'll ever become whole again to listening to the pickiest customers and employees who spend their entire day talking about basically nothing.

"It was really good seeing you again," Evie says, grabbing the pickup ticket I just placed in front of her.

"Yeah, it was good seeing you too." And it's the truth. Even though I fight the twinge in my gut and the slight race of my pulse each time I'm around her, I'm very aware that it's there. I just don't know what to do about it. Because this is not the time in my life for me to be attracted to anyone.

Evie puts her ticket into the pocket of her lab jacket as she turns to walk away, and I suddenly realize I don't want her to leave. "Your clothes will be ready by the end of the week."

She stops and turns to face me. "It's no rush. I spend more time in scrubs than real clothes." She laughs. "I'll probably pick them up in a couple of weeks." Evie turns away from me, grabs the door handle, and pulls it open.

My heart beats a little harder as she takes her first step over the threshold. "Hey, Evie, hold up a second." I move quickly around the counter as she stops and releases the door. I can't believe I'm about to do this, but for some reason, I think I'll live to regret it if I don't because this may be the last time I see her since I'm fairly sure I won't be here in two weeks when she stops by to pick up her clothes. "Have you eaten dinner yet?" I'm not really sure where those words came from, but it doesn't matter because the question is out there floating around between us.

"Um…no." She leans against the wall next to the door, her focus never leaving me.

SIX

Evie

———

I KNOW where he's headed with his question, and I'm both confused and irritated. Confused because he seems like he has a lot going on to want to start something new. *He's probably just looking for a friend, Evie. Don't get your hopes up.* And irritated because of the timing of our third encounter. I'll admit I've thought about him often over the past few months after taking care of him that night in the hospital. He was discharged the following day, so by the time I returned to work seven nights later, he was long gone.

I'd hoped his treatments were going well and that he would make a full recovery because, as a nurse, that's what I wish for all of my patients, but there's always been something different about Bennett. Maybe it's because he was the first guy I met after coming off one of the worst breakups of my life. It was New Year's Day, and we were both drinking the magic whiskey and hoping for better days ahead. But after taking care of him in the hospital, I had a lot more clarity on why he had been so down. He had cancer and he honestly thought he was dying, and that's exactly what he told me. Then I basically told him he needed to seek out help for his mental condition. *I'm a terrible person.*

His brown eyes darken a bit as a small smile tugs at the corners of his mouth. It's just enough to give me a glimpse of his dimples. God, I'm a sucker for this brown-eyed guy with dimples. All he has to do is smile and I turn to mush—which is exactly what I'm trying to avoid right now because there is absolutely no way I'm going to be able to give him the answer we both want.

"Do you want to grab something to eat?" He's nervous. It's evident on his face and in his voice. He hesitates a beat, but his attention never wavers from me. "I need to make sure all the equipment is off and everything is locked up, and then we can leave." He licks his lips quickly before a small smile returns to his face.

I want to say yes so badly—so, so badly—but it all goes back to timing. Terrible timing. If I'd just waited until tomorrow to drop my clothes off, I would've been able to say yes. *But what if he's not working here tomorrow?*

"I can't. I mean I really want to, but I'm on my way to work."

His smile slowly fades. "Of course you are." He shakes his head. "You work nights and it's…" He nods toward the window, which reveals the darkening sky. "Nighttime. I understand. Just—"

"Bad timing," I interject quickly, cutting him off before he finishes his sentence.

"Yeah, bad timing." He rubs the back of his neck and releases a long slow breath. "Maybe some other time."

"Yes, definitely another time," I say quickly, but what I really want to ask is when some other time will be. I don't ask, though, because I don't want to appear desperate or needy. Instead I just toss the ball back in his court. "You have my number, so you can give me a call or shoot me a text when you want to grab a bite." There. Now he can think about it and decide if he really wants to take me to dinner or if this was just an impulsive whim.

He narrows his eyes a bit. "Your number?"

"I gave it to you when you were checking in my clothes." Wow. How quickly he forgot. Yeah, he's not gonna call, and that thought makes me a bit sad.

Bennett nods slowly. "Right. I'll give you a call," he says, not so convincingly.

"Don't forget we always have next year—New Year's Day at The Red Door, 10:00 A.M." *God, I sound needy and creepy and a whole lot pathetic.*

"Yeah, it's a date." And with those four words, I turn and walk out the door.

I do...

SEVEN

October
————

Evie

"I DO," my best friend, Jade, whispers to her soon-to-be husband Brock. I can hear everything, including her soft sniffles as Brock says his vows and the preacher says all the sweet and sappy shit about love and forever. Anyway, the reason I can decipher every word spoken so easily is because I'm one of her bridesmaids—the maid of honor, to be exact, so I'm actually only standing about three steps away from her. Jade has been my best friend for most of my life, and she met Brock six months ago then got engaged two months later, and four months after she said yes, we're all standing here inside this small chapel wondering what the hell she was thinking. Well, everybody may not be wondering that, but I sure am. She told me after her first date that Brock was the man she was going to marry. When I laughed and told her there was no way she was going to marry some uptight rich guy who crunches numbers all day at his father's accounting firm, she simply laughed and said watch me. And that's exactly what I'm doing—watching her marry the uptight number cruncher. But hey, if she's happy, more power to her.

After the preacher presents them as husband and wife, the small crowd of weddinggoers cheers and applauds before heading out of the chapel toward where the real fun begins: The Rant, the best wedding reception venue in Riverport. A lot of couples have their weddings here at The Wedding Bell Chapel and then move their guests about a block down the well-lit sidewalk to the reception. The Rant and The Wedding Bell are the perfect combination. Jade opted not to have a huge wedding, hence me being the only bridesmaid and Brock's brother being his best man. Or it could possibly be that she only had four months to plan the wedding, which didn't give her enough time to have the big affair she'd always dreamed of. Either way I think every-thing worked out perfectly. She put all of her time, energy, and money into the huge reception, because that's what she said was ultimately important to her. I, on the other hand, used to dream of a huge ceremony without even any thought of a reception. But since my ex, Kyle, decided he'd rather marry Lori, my stepsister, instead of me—the girl he dated for six years and lived with for three—it kind of shut down all my hopes and dreams of ever getting married at all. I shake my head a couple of times and push all thoughts of Kyle and Lori from my head because neither are worth my energy. And more importantly, tonight is about Jade and Brock's future and not my shitty past.

I meet the best man in the center of the aisle, looping my arm in his, and we walk quickly toward the double doors at the back of the chapel.

"Do you want to ride with me to the reception and I can bring you back to your car afterward, or give you a lift home depending on how much you have to drink?" Tony, Brock's younger brother, offers.

"No thanks. It's nice outside, so I think I'll just walk." And good try on securing the early-before-the-drinking-starts hookup, which is not happening with him or anybody else. Since Kyle, I haven't been interested in dating or hooking up with anybody. I'm not sure if it's because we were together for so long or the fact that he cheated me and I'm just not sure if my heart can take another round of pounding from anyone. In other words, I'm a little unsure of letting my guard down even though it's been almost a year since he turned my life upside down.

"If you change your mind…" Tony winks and then tosses me what I assume to be his signature smirk. I'm not attracted to him, his wink, or his smirk. So even if I were itching to hook up tonight, it wouldn't be with him.

"I won't, but thank you." I'm really trying to be nice to this guy because he's now a part of Jade's family and I'll probably be seeing him from time to time.

"Do you have your phone?" His green eyes widen as he leans in a bit closer to me. *Please just stop already.*

"Do you see what I'm wearing?" I spin around once and stop when I'm facing him again. "Where would I put a phone in this dress?" *And even if I did have it, I wouldn't let you put your number in.*

"I wasn't sure if there was maybe some compartment sewed in there somewhere for a cell phone." He hesitates a second. "I was going to offer you my number in case you change your mind."

I take a step away from him. "Look, Tony, we're going to be at the same reception, and the building is not so big that I wouldn't be able to find you if I wanted to. But see, the thing is—" I stop mid-sentence because I'm about to be really rude and possibly hurt his feelings. But damn, what do I have to do to make him understand that he and I are not happening, not tonight or any other night?

"Tony, hey, man, I thought that was you." A familiar voice yanks me away from my thoughts.

Tony's gaze leaves me and lands on the guy who just walked up to us and is standing next to him. "Yeah, it's me. Oh, hey, how are doing, man? It's been a while, huh?" Tony responds, and my gaze travels to the tall dark-haired guy standing next him. *Bennett.*

I'm met with not one but two equally sexy dimples as Bennett smiles, but unfortunately the smile isn't for me; it's for Tony. Fucking Tony. I've suddenly changed my whole outlook on life. Maybe a hookup isn't such a bad idea. Maybe I am ready to get back in the proverbial saddle, just not with Tony. *Don't get your hopes up, Evie—remember it was just a few months ago when Bennett said he'd call but didn't.* It's also my fault because I turned him down when he asked me out to dinner. *But I had to work.* Dammit! I wish my heart and my head would stop battling over who's to blame, because what's important right now is that Bennett is standing just a few feet away from me.

I clear my throat, which is not very ladylike and extremely sad. But who cares? Bennett looks good—so good. Better than he did the morning I met him at The Red Door.

Tony's eyes dart to me. "Are you okay?"

I guess the throat clearing was a good idea after all. "Yeah, I'm fine. I'm just going to head over to the reception now." I smile then take a quick look over at a wide-eyed Bennett. I wonder if he was at the wedding. How does he know Tony? Why hasn't he said anything to me? So many questions for a man I barely know.

"Yeah, okay. See you there." *Don't count on it.*

I smile at Bennett before walking away.

EIGHT

Bennett

EVIE IS BEAUTIFUL. Her red hair is piled high on top of her head in a tight bun. Her dark eyes are bright, and the cut of the dress she's wearing shows off the slight curve of her neck. Damn, she's not only beautiful but sexy too.

She walks away from us, and I try not to stare at the sway of her hips in the snug-fitting blue dress. Instead I direct my attention toward Tony and ask the question that's weighing heavy on my mind. "How long have you two been dating?" I'm not sure how old Evie is, but Tony is fairly young, probably early twenties. I'm not sure if he's even graduated from college yet. It doesn't really matter, but it's just that I would think Evie would be more likely to be in a relationship with someone who is more settled since she has her own career.

Tony chuckles. "We're not. I don't date—not my style. You know I'm more of the love 'em and leave 'em type."

I shake my head. "No, I don't know." How fucking cheesy is this guy? "Does Evie know what your plans are?" The curiosity is killing me. I'd hope she wouldn't fall for Tony's shit.

He takes another step closer to me and grins. "No, and that's the plan. Man, you know you can't tell a chick you're gonna fuck her and walk. That's not cool," he whispers.

What a little shit. "What's not cool is lying to get laid. You'd be surprised how many women want the same thing as you." I shake my head. "But what you're doing is a dick move if you ask me." *He didn't ask, but somebody needs to set this kid straight.*

"Don't tell me you've never lied to a chick to get laid." Tony laughs.

Memories flood my mind of all the one-night stands I've had, which is actually not too many, and the answer is no. "I didn't have to lie because we came to an agreement up front. That way there's never any miscommunication. Then if she decides she doesn't want what I do, we go our separate ways."

"Yeah, okay, man. Whatever you say." Tony laughs again. "So how do you know Evie anyway?"

I think about the day I met her at The Red Door. She was annoyingly adorable. But then when she was my nurse, she was quiet and caring. And the last time I saw her, I lied to her, but it wasn't to fuck with her; it was to protect her from my shitty life. I wasn't ready to go on a date with her that night at the cleaners; I only asked on impulse. Then I told her I'd call, but I didn't. Does that make me a liar? Deep down inside, I wanted to call her, to ask her out to dinner again, but I couldn't because I wasn't ready then. Now things are different. So much different. I feel better about my battle more than ever. I've won. At least I feel like I've won. "She took care of me when I was in the hospital a few months ago."

"So are you doing okay? I see your hair's grown back." He nods toward my head.

"I'm good. A lot better than I was back at the first of the year." I'm beginning to feel like my life is getting back to normal. I'm finished with my treatments, I've gained back some of the weight I lost, my hair has grown in, and I'm getting ready to head back to work tomorrow.

"Good to hear it, man. It's really good to hear it," Tony says sincerely.

A young blonde woman walks past us. She looks over her shoulder at Tony and smiles.

"Hey, man, look," he says, "it was good to see you, but I need to get over to the reception." He smiles toward the blonde. "Are you gonna be there? I'm sure my brother would like to see you."

I haven't seen Brock in a long time. When my family got the invitation to the reception, I volunteered to come because Tess is busy with her family, and ever since my dad died, my mom avoids these types of functions. Right now, after seeing Evie, I'm glad I agreed to come.

"Yep. I'm actually heading that way now."

Tony nods slightly. "My family's probably wondering where I'm at, so I'll see you later," he says as he rushes away from me, falling in step with the blonde.

NINE

Evie

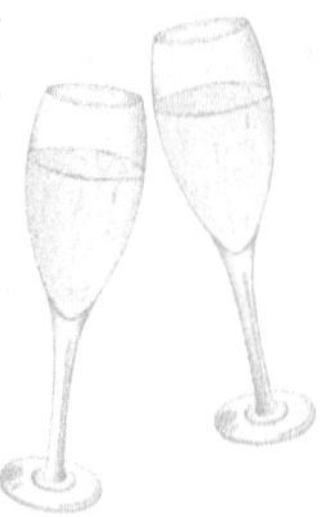

"YOU LOOK BEAUTIFUL TONIGHT." Bennett's warm breath brushes over my neck. My heart skips a beat as his words roll around in my head. *He thinks I'm beautiful.* I take a sip from the champagne flute I'm holding before turning to face him. My eyes flit to his and he smiles immediately.

"Thank you. You look handsome yourself." His smile grows wider before he briefly looks away. I hope I didn't embarrass him, but damn, this guy is more than handsome. He looks healthy and happy, two things I've never seen on him before.

"Thanks. How are you?" he asks as he pushes his hands into the front pockets of his dress slacks.

"I'm good, and from where I'm standing, you look like you're doing pretty well too." I take another sip of champagne.

"I am doing well. I've actually just been released to go back to work. So, I guess you could say my life is returning to normal." His dimples make another quick appearance before he licks his lips.

"That's great, Bennett. I'm so happy for you." And I mean it, because I'm not petty about things like him never calling me even after he told me he would. I'm sure he had his reasons.

"So, do you know the groom?" I ask, attempting to change the subject.

"Yeah, Brock's father's accounting firm handles financial stuff for the cleaners."

I nod and take a final gulp of champagne to finish off glass number two. I'm not sure if I need any more considering the way my skin tingles and my heart races just being near Bennett. *It's got to be the alcohol.*

"Jade, his wife, is my best friend," I tell him as I slip my empty champagne flute onto the tray of a passing waiter.

"Huh, small world." He laughs.

"Yep, it is. Didn't we already determine it's a small world the last time we spoke?"

"We did." His gaze leaves mine briefly as he surveys the large room.

Bennett's focus quickly returns to me before he leans in a bit closer. Goose bumps dance across my skin as he whispers near my ear. "Walk with me." He pulls away from me slightly and motions toward the French doors in the back of the room.

"Okay." Luckily, my voice didn't sound the way I feel—unsure, nervous, jittery.

I walk next to him as we make our way across the room, maneuvering through the crowd. He opens the door and steps back for me to walk through first. *Such a gentleman.* He falls in step beside me as we walk over to the railing that overlooks a large, well-lit outside dance floor. There's a band, a bar, and a lot of people, but there's enough distance between us and them that I can barely hear the music.

"Have I told you how beautiful you look tonight?" He smiles again, giving me yet another peek at those dimples. God, I wish he'd stop teasing me.

Heat flushes over my face. "Stop. You're embarrassing me." It's true. For some reason, compliments always tend to mess with my head, I guess maybe because I'm not used to men saying nice things to me. Kyle was always such an asshole, and for some fucked-up reason, I liked it. Or at least I thought I did. He was rough around the edges, but not necessarily in a good way. He had an amazing body and a rugged face. He was the ultimate bad boy. In other words, I let myself get wrapped up in a guy who was beautiful on the outside but ugly on the inside. I let that guy manipulate me and treat me like shit. Kyle leaving me homeless and broke was the best thing he could have done. It's given me time to pull my life back together and learn to love myself again.

"I'm not telling you that repeatedly to embarrass you, Evie. It's just every time I look at you, you're more beautiful than the time before."

"Seriously, you've got to stop." *Because if you don't, I'm going to either combust from all the heat rushing to my face or melt into a puddle at your feet.*

He grins. "Okay, I'll stop…under one condition."

I lean in a little closer to him. "What's that?"

"You dance with me."

My heart free-falls into my stomach. I can't dance. Not at all. "What if I say no?"

"You won't." He takes a step toward me, standing so close I can feel the heat radiating from his body.

"I might." Any confidence I had earlier is gone, but he doesn't need to know that. How did our innocent conversation become this? Dancing? Nausea hits me hard. My hands are sweaty, and my chest is tight. The last time I danced in public was three years ago, at a concert with my ex. I was drunk. He was drunk. But none of that matters because he humiliated me in front of all our friends. Later he apologized and blamed the alcohol. It doesn't matter how much you've had to drink; mean words still hurt.

I glance over my shoulder at all the couples dancing. Maybe I should tell him the truth so he knows why I won't dance in public. If I do that, then perhaps he'll stop asking.

"Hey, Evie," Bennett says as he hooks his finger under my chin and brings my focus back to him.

"Yeah?" I blink a couple of times before forcing a smile.

"I don't want to go out there." He motions toward the dance floor. "We can dance here."

My nervousness ramps up considerably, because dancing on a semi-crowded dance floor would make my inability to dance much less conspicuous than being the lone couple dancing on the patio.

"Here?" I'm getting really good at one-word responses.

"Yeah, here. Just you and me under the light of the moon." He grins, pointing up toward the sky.

I shrug. "I don't know." *Just be honest with the man. Tell him you can't dance.* He reaches for my hand and I pull it away from him.

"Look, Bennett, I can't dance, and it makes me uncomfortable to try. Especially if a lot of people are watching."

He places his hand at the small of my back and edges me away from the railing. I reluctantly go with him. He doesn't speak, but he's sporting that dimpled smile I like far too much. I tear my eyes away from his face because I don't want anything about our time together to give him the idea that I'm a weirdo creeper who can't stop ogling him. Once we make it around the side of the building, he stops and turns to face me. "Is this better?"

I take in the dimly lit sidewalk surrounded by a large, beautifully landscaped yard with a swimming pool, a hot tub, and a club house. The one thing I don't see are people. Not one single person. Only us. I know what he's doing, and it's working.

"Better for what?" I ask playfully.

My heart skips a beat as he leans in closer and whispers near my ear. "For this." His warm lips brush against my neck as he laces his fingers through mine.

"Wait, what?" My pulse begins to race when he wraps his arm around my waist, squeezes my hand gently, and then pulls me flush against his body. *Oh. My. God.* A thousand butterflies take flight in my stomach as we begin to move, slowly swaying to the beat of the distant music. I'm dizzy with emotions…too many emotions to actually decipher which ones are giving me all the crazy feelings exploding inside of me.

"I thought you said you couldn't dance," Bennett says as he dips me slightly and looks into my eyes. I'm dead—or at least I'm dying, because this moment feels so damn real.

He gently lifts me back up to a standing position and my gaze meets his. "I can't. This is all you." I smile.

"If you say so." His dimples make another quick appearance, and I force myself to forget about how much I want to touch them—with my tongue. God, there is something seriously wrong with me. This guy has just gone through the fight of his life and all I can think about is licking his dimples.

I smile before resting my head against his chest. His nearness is causing my senses to spin. Out. Of. Control. How can I let this happen? Allow him to affect me like this? I barely know him. I have to back away and give myself some room to breathe in something other than his strong masculine scent. Luckily, my timing is perfect because the band stops playing and announces a ten-minute break.

I pull away from his hold and tilt my head back until my eyes meet his. "You're different." So different, even from the first time I met him.

"Different?" He chuckles. "I'm not different, Evie. The person you see tonight is the real Bennett Stern. The man you first met at The Red Door on New Year's Day thought he was dying. He didn't believe it was fair to introduce you to what his life was about to become." He leans down and kisses my forehead gently.

I never really thought about it like that. I can see where being diagnosed with cancer can change a person. I'm happy he's been able to find his way back to who he was before and not let that horrible disease change his life forever.

"What about the guy in the hospital or the guy at the cleaners? Was that not the real Bennett Stern?" I pull back a little more until his hand drops from my waist.

"The guy in the hospital was depressed and embarrassed to appear so weak he couldn't even go through chemotherapy treatment without ending up in a hospital bed with something as simple as dehydration."

"Bennett…" My heart hurts so much for him. I certainly didn't want him to relive the last few months of his life tonight when he seems so happy and upbeat.

"Please let me finish." His voice is calm, his gaze steady.

I nod, and then bite at my bottom lip as I wait for him to continue.

"Then the day I saw you at the cleaners, I was surprised, but at the same time happy to see you again. Even so, I still wasn't sure I was ready to grab ahold of my life and move on. I still had so much doubt and fear for the future and didn't want to wrap you up in my problems."

"So that's why you didn't call?" I get it. I really do. But I still have trust issues that go deep, and lying is something I can't deal with—not that he's asking me to be in a relationship. I'm so out of practice with this boy-meets-girl bullshit.

He nods and then looks to the sky. *Shit!* Maybe I'm pushing too hard, or being too blunt. I just don't know and feel like I need to be honest, because that's what I want. Honesty.

"Yeah, that's mostly the reason," he says as his focus

returns to me. "I was so hesitant about asking you to dinner in the first place because I really didn't think I was ready."

"For dinner?" I laugh, trying to lighten up the mood a little.

He chuckles. "I was feeling a hell of a lot better, and it just happened. I mean the words just came out of my mouth before I had time to really think about whether or not I was ready. I've thought about you so much since that day at the cleaners, but after a week or so passed, I was afraid it was too late to call." He shakes his head. "I should have called you, Evie. Even if it was to tell you I wasn't ready. I'm really sorry. Can you forgive me?" He shifts his weight slightly and gently pulls me back flush against his body.

"I already have," I whisper.

Bennett holds me tight for a few minutes, neither of us moving. Only the soft sounds of our breathing and the distant noise of the party surround us. I'm content and happy in this moment and hope this is the beginning of something beautiful.

He pulls back slightly. "You know after that day at the cleaners, I remembered that no matter what happened, I'd see you again on New Year's Day." He's swaying again, but this time there's no music.

"New Year's Day?" I pretend not to know what he's talking about, but in reality, I know exactly what he's referring to. I just want to hear him say it.

"You don't remember. Man, am I that forgettable?" He steps away from me and I immediately miss his nearness, his touch, his scent. I miss him.

"Not a chance. I just needed to hear you say it." I place my hand on his forearm.

He covers my hand with his and takes a step toward me, his gaze never leaving mine. "If you're still living around here next year, meet me back at The Red Door on New Year's Day, same time."

"Okay, it's a date," I say, smiling just before he presses his lips to mine.

Happy New Year!

TEN

New Year's Eve

Bennett

WHEN I TEXTED Evie and asked her to meet me at my sister's New Year's Eve party, I didn't think she would. I haven't seen her since the night of her best friend's wedding, but we've been texting or talking on the phone almost every night, mostly because I've been working my ass off. I've been traveling for the last three months with only two stops back home. Both times Evie was working, and we didn't have time to meet up. That's one reason why tonight is so important. It'll be the first time I've seen her in what feels like forever.

I make my way through my sister's living room and into the kitchen. Evie's back is to me as she chats someone up. I chuckle to myself as I watch her do what she does best—talk. She's moving her hands and shifting her weight around as she speaks, and it reminds me of the first time we met.

Lucky for me, over the past few months, she's become a part of my life that I need and count on. Her voice at the end of a long day gives me hope that my days are going to be brighter and better, because of her.

I move in behind her and rest my hands on her hips. Her body jerks slightly before she looks over her shoulder at me. A small smile tugs at the corners of her mouth as she drags her hand over the scruff on my face. "Hey, you," she says softly, her eyes widening. "I really like the new look." My dick twitches behind my zipper as she continues to move her hand over my face. It's been far too long since I've had a woman's hands on me. I gently grab her wrist and move her hand because my dick getting hard in front of Tess and her friends is not what I have planned for tonight.

"It's about time you show your ugly face." My sister's voice is loud and clear, and she is most likely standing directly behind me.

"I got here as soon as I could." I say the words to Evie, completely ignoring Tess.

"It's fine. I've had a lot of fun. I already know your sister, and I actually ran into a couple more people I knew." Evie stands on her tiptoes and kisses my cheek. That simple kiss reminds me of the night of Brock and Jade's wedding. We made out behind that dimly lit building for almost an hour. I swear it felt like we were a couple of teenagers who wanted more but were both scared to make the first move.

"I'm really glad you're here now." Evie smiles and slips her hand in mine.

"Yeah, me too."

"Blah, blah, blah. Did you forget about me?" Tess asks as she maneuvers her body around us until she's standing in front of me.

"How could I forget about you with that loud mouth?" I joke.

Tess moves in closer and gives me a quick one-armed hug. "I'm glad you're home," she tells me before her eyes flit to Evie and she smiles. "You two have fun tonight." Tess winks and then walks away.

"You heard her—we have to have fun tonight. It's an order from the hostess," Evie says, gently squeezing my hand.

"So, we have an hour before midnight. What do you want to do? Hang out here with a bunch of people we don't really know or head back to my place and make out like teenagers again?" I hope she picks option two, because I need some alone time with her. Months of talking to her but not being able to hold her or kiss her has made me crazy with need. Now that I feel like life has given me the green light to start living, that's exactly what I want to do.

"Hmm…" She taps her finger against her chin. "Stay here with all the drunks or hide out at your place and…what was that you said we could do?" She laughs.

"Make out like teenagers." I answer her quickly and smile, giving her a glimpse of my dimples, praying that will persuade her to get the hell out of here.

"Does that include kissing and touching and possibly getting naked?" She licks her lips then presses them together.

"Sweetheart, it includes anything you want to do." My heart pounds in my chest and my erection presses against my zipper. We've got to get out of here because neither my heart nor my dick can take her teasing.

She rises to her toes, and I lean in closer. Her lips brush my neck before she softly whispers, "I choose kissing and touching." Her breath is warm against my skin as she nibbles at my ear. "And getting naked. I choose going to your place and getting naked." Evie pulls away from me and her dark eyes find mine. "Is that okay with you?" She lifts her eyebrows and presses her lips together.

I adjust the growing beast in my jeans and lead her away from the kitchen, through the living room, and out the front door. As soon as we're outside, I guide her to my truck, only to stop before opening the door.

"In case you're wondering—yes, it's okay with me." I cover her mouth with mine and kiss her for not nearly as long as I want to, but I know the best part of tonight is yet to come.

ELEVEN

Evie

WE CAN'T GET inside his house fast enough, at least not fast enough for me. I've never wanted to be with someone as much as I do Bennett. I think the three months of nothing but conversation, whether it be texting, FaceTime, or talking, was good for us. We grew from not really knowing each other to becoming something more, so much more. But, what we are is hard to explain because we've had very little physical interaction, other than the night of Jade's wedding and about five minutes ago when we sucked face in front of his sister's house. I don't know about him, but I can't wait.

We've had more than enough foreplay. I just want his dick inside of me.

The front door shuts behind us and I grab him, slamming his body against the wall. I slant my mouth over his and kiss him hard and wild. I'm not sure who I've become tonight, but Bennett's not complaining.

The heat inside me flares as he cups my ass and I immediately fall against him. He's touching me, holding me, keeping close. So fucking close, but it's not enough.

"More, I need more." My words come out on a whisper, and Bennett doesn't hesitate. He lifts me from the floor, and I wrap my legs around his waist, bringing my soaked panties flush with his erection. I grind and roll my hips because it feels so damn good. I mean better than good. He kisses me hard and holds me tight until we make it to the second door on the left, which I'm assuming is his bedroom.

"How much more do you want?" Bennett whispers near my ear as he lays me across the soft mattress. He quickly climbs onto the bed and hovers over me, our bodies near but not quite touching. His eyes darken before he kisses me fiercely, leaving my mouth and my pussy on fire.

I let out a long slow moan as he brushes his lips over mine one last time before pulling away. "Don't stop. I want it all." My words are the truth, the way I feel—the way I haven't felt in so long.

"Are you sure?" he asks, his brown eyes growing darker.

I nod. "Yes."

Bennett rises slightly and tears off his t-shirt. My hands itch to touch him, all of him, but he's suddenly gone. I rise up on my elbows and search the barely lit room for him. He's not hard to find because he's standing directly in front of me completely naked except for his dark boxer briefs. His body is perfect. Hard planes, toned abs, and muscular legs. He's been taking care of himself, and that alone puts a smile on my face.

"If you want it all, then why are you the only one still dressed?" He grins as he opens the drawer to his nightstand and grabs a condom.

"I was too busy staring at you standing naked in front of me." Heat rushes to my face with my admission.

"So, do you like what you see?" he teases.

"Not sure…you'll need to come a little closer and let me get a better look." I sit up and scoot toward the edge of the bed. Bennett tosses the condom on the comforter next to me and drops to his knees. He gently removes my black boots then grips my legs and tugs me closer to him. I'm met with a huge bulge still tucked snugly away in a pair of boxer briefs. I tilt my head back slightly until my eyes meet his.

"Touch me, Evie." He licks his lips, and his brown eyes darken.

My nerves kick in—hard. It's been over a year since I've had sex, and I wrestle with the possibility that our first time together may not be what he's expecting. What if it's terrible and he backs out of whatever it is we have before giving it a chance to even get started? No! I will not go there. Bennett is not that guy. He's not mean or arrogant or an asshole. He's kind and caring and is so thankful to be alive that he celebrates almost daily that he's been given another chance to live his life.

I swallow hard as I wrap my hands around his rock-hard thighs and pull him in closer to me. I lean in and cover his underwear-covered erection with my mouth. His cock is so damn hard. Bennett releases a long slow moan as I drag my tongue over his shaft before gently pressing my teeth against his length. He twitches under my touch and it's so fucking hot. My mouth travels a bit higher and stops just above the waistband of his briefs. I kiss and nibble at his warm skin as he rocks his hips slightly.

"Fuck, Evie. I can't do this. It's been too long." His voice is soft and shaky. Bennett cups my face and tilts my head back slightly. My eyes flit to his, and that's all it takes. He needs this as much as I do. I can see it. On his face. In his whiskey-colored eyes. He wants me.

"Me either. Me too," I whisper, mostly to myself, but it's true. All the teasing and foreplay can wait for next time. *Don't get too presumptuous, Evie. What if this is the only time?* I shake the negativity out of my head and focus on the here and now, and what I need right now is him hovering over me, pushing his hard cock deep inside of me then pulling out slowly and doing it again. Pushing and pulling, over and over again until I'm screaming his name.

Bennett gently grabs my arms, helping me stand. His hands work quickly as he pulls my red sweater dress over my head and lets it fall to the floor. A shiver rocks through me as I realize I'm standing almost naked in front of him, a guy I barely know yet feel like I've known for a lifetime.

He blows out a slow breath as he surveys me from head to toe. He doesn't speak a word as he drops to his knees and slowly slides my black panties away from my hips and down my legs. His warm breath skims over my skin, and then a thousand goose bumps follow. Bennett's lips move across my stomach and over my right hip. A shudder races up my spine as his mouth continues to travel to places that have been untouched by a man for so damn long. His tongue licks my center once and then again. My legs grow weak, and he must sense it somehow because he cups my ass with his strong hands, as I begin thrusting my hips. I drop my head back and bite my lip to keep from screaming. Because his tongue dancing around my clit is driving me crazy.

"Evie, baby, you taste sweeter than you smell." His words brush against my sensitive skin sending a shiver up my spine.

I bring my head back to center and gently run my fingers through his thick hair. Bennett moans against my clit, and I swear I almost come. My fingers twitch to try that little move again, and my girly bits are in complete agreement. I tug at his dark hair a couple of times before sliding my fingers through his thick locks. He moans again and again as my fingers massage his scalp. Bennett's moan is followed by a lick and then a gentle teeth tug at my clit. He continues to lick and tug over and over again until I see stars. I call out his name as my orgasm hits me hard. All the air leaves my lungs and I swear I can't breathe. I grab the comforter and roll my hips, giving way to the feeling that follows. Ecstasy. Pure ecstasy.

As my breathing begins to return to normal, my gaze flits to the sexy guy on his knees in front of me. The nervousness I felt earlier jars me again as his eyes find mine. He smiles before kissing my left hip softly. He's quickly scatters more kisses across my stomach until he reaches my right hip.

"I'm ready for more, Evie," Bennett whispers as he pushes off the floor and stands in front of me.

"Me too," I say softly.

I slip my shaky fingers into the waistband of his boxer briefs and tug them down, away from his hips, down his muscular legs until they're in a puddle at his feet. I lick my lips and reach for his erection, but he stops me before I'm able to taste him. My face flushes a bit as my breath catches. I'm embarrassed. Why did he stop me? I mean, what kind of man pulls back on the reins when he's about to get a blow job? Especially if it's really been as long for him as it has for me. I move my hand from his cock and drop my eyes toward the floor. I just wanted to give him what he gave me.

"Hey, Evie, I'm up here." His voice is soft and kind, but still full of need.

I slowly look up at him and he helps me stand.

Bennett reaches around me and unhooks my bra, and it falls to the floor. His eyes darken as he takes in my body. I'm completely naked. There's nothing between us anymore.

"Let's save that for later because I want you so fucking bad that I can't wait." A smile pulls at his lips. "And plus, I wouldn't make it more than a few seconds, and that's not what I want you to remember about tonight." He gently grips my face before covering my mouth with his. His kiss is deep, robbing the air from my lungs.

I close my eyes and live in this moment. Me and him. The accidental relationship I never saw coming.

Bennett pulls away from our kiss. "I need you, Evie. Now," he says, stepping out of his underwear. He climbs onto the bed and then reaches for me. My heart flipflops in my chest as I follow him without any hesitation.

He kisses me slowly as his body falls against mine.

"Is this what you want?" he asks, briefly pulling away from our kiss.

"Yes." *More than anything.*

Bennett straddles me and sits back on his haunches before grabbing the condom. He rips open the foil packet, removes the latex, and rolls it over his cock.

Heat licks at my cheeks as I take in all of Bennett. He's healthy and strong and so damn sexy. He rises to his knees, gives me a full dimpled smile, and then nudges my legs farther apart.

"Come here," I whisper, reaching for him.

Bennett shifts his weight slightly, hovering over me. "I'm right here." He kisses my shoulder and then my neck. His erection pushes at my entrance just as a full-body shudder rips through me. *I want this so much.*

He doesn't rush, but he's not exactly taking his time either as he thrusts deep inside of me. Bennett rocks his hips, pushing his thickness even deeper.

"You feel so damn good." His breathing is choppy as he lets out a long, slow moan.

"So good," I hum, my lips grazing his.

Bennett pulls back slowly and then plunges into me hard. He does it again. And again. The bed jerks beneath us, but he doesn't stop. He continues to push and pull. Plunge and withdraw. I can't breathe, but I don't care. This moment feels too good to care. He's here with me, not a hundred miles away working. He's healthy and happy and so full of energy. And when he comes, it sets off a fire in me like I've never felt before. My body shakes and shudders as my own orgasm takes me to a place that hangs between fantasy and reality. A place where broken hearts are mended and the possibility of a brighter future is within my grasp. Everything seems to happen fast—too fast. I don't want it to be over, but it is.

Bennett rests his head against mine for a couple of seconds before kissing the tip of my nose. "I don't want to move," he whispers against my mouth.

His lips are soft, tempting, and I moan softly. "Then don't. Stay here." *Forever.*

He tugs me against him, rolling us over a bit until we're spooning. I fight a laugh because I've never let another guy hold me like this, especially after sex. I'm usually out of bed and in the bathroom cleaning up immediately. Then when I return, I crawl into my spot and fall asleep without any cuddling. But tonight is different. Bennett is different, and I'm different with him.

"Happy New Year," he says with a slight chuckle.

"Oh my God! I completely forgot about—never mind. Happy New Year." I wriggle my bottom against him.

"Hey now, none of that or you're going to wake the beast. Unless that's what you want…" He rises up above me, and I tilt my head back so I can focus on his face.

"Maybe I do want." I smile, and he presses a quick kiss to my lips.

"Was I really so good you forgot about it being New Year's Eve?" he teases.

"You were definitely distracting." *Very distracting.*

Bennett relaxes against me and places his lips against my shoulder. For the first time in a really long time, my mind is clear, the air surrounding me is peaceful, and my body is at ease.

TWELVE

Evie

I AWAKE with a startle and immediately sit up. My surroundings are unfamiliar. I know where I am, it's just that last night it was much darker. I survey Bennett's rather large bedroom and am amazed at how put together and beautiful it is. The walls are brown with hanging lights on each side of the bed. The bay window to my right gives way to a lot of morning light. Thank God it appears to be facing the backyard, which is shut off to the outside world with a privacy fence. I check out the empty spot next to me and notice my phone. I close my eyes for a beat and try to remember if I left it there. *Nope, because that spot was occupied*

by Bennett, who is no longer here. I drag my hand over the empty side of the bed. It's cold, which means he's been gone for a while. The house is completely silent, which confirms that I'm more than likely alone.

I'm not upset. He'll be back. *Of course he will, because he lives here.* I unlock the screen on my phone to check the time. It's only seven thirty. Where the hell would he have gone so early? I run all the possible scenarios through my head, and I get nothing. He's not at work. He didn't mention any kind of appointment today. Rather than drive myself crazy over Bennett not being in bed with me, I decide to text him. If he's somewhere in the house, we'll both have a good laugh and go on with our day.

Me: Hey! Just woke up alone. Wondering where you are. 😊

I choose the smiley face emoji over the sad face so I don't look needy and insecure. Because I'm not. Damn you, Kyle, for making me so damn untrusting.

So, I wait. I stare at the screen for what feels like an hour. No text. Nothing. I take a deep breath and slowly blow it out. Now, I have to decide if I wait until he comes home or leave and save myself the embarrassment of still being here when he walks through the front door.

I climb out of bed and get dressed. After I pull my boots on and grab my phone, I make my way down the hall and into the kitchen. No coffee or breakfast waiting on me. I check the refrigerator door, the table, and the countertops, but there's no note anywhere. I should've known not to get so wrapped up in the first guy who showed me a little bit of attention. I'm an idiot. Tears fill my eyes, but I don't cry. I'm not about to cry over some guy I hardly know. *But I do know him. I know him well, and that's what makes this entire situation hard for me to understand.*

I open the screen of my phone and order an Uber. I just want to go home, because sitting around here and waiting for him to return is not something I want to do today.

Once my car is on its way, I head outside, because staying in here makes me think of him, and right now, that's not where I want my head to be.

New Year's Day

Evie

THE RED DOOR glares at me.

Mocking.

Laughing.

Taunting.

I glance down at my watch. It's 10:00 A.M. It's been exactly one year since I last walked over the threshold of The Red Door Bar. My life has changed so much, and only twenty-four hours ago, I thought I had it all. I was happy. I'd recovered from the humiliation and hurt of what Kyle had done to me. I'd discovered that a guy who didn't have tattoos or treat me like shit could make me feel things I'd never felt before.

Happiness.

Contentment.

Bliss.

My life was better than it's ever been, at least until I realized what had happened. I had allowed myself to fall in love with a man who was fighting a battle so much stronger than anything we had become. Even so, I'm still here standing outside the bar where it all began. It's my last-ditch effort to prove to myself that it was real. That we were real. We. Are. Real.

The wind picks up, and I tilt my head back, taking in the dark clouds. A single snowflake hits my face. *Not again.* Two years in a row isn't a miracle—it's downright weird and somewhat nerve-racking. I shake my head and pull the door open, stepping inside the dimly lit room. I slowly scan the space before allowing my gaze to find the bar. I pull in a much-needed deep breath as my eyes flit from one empty stool to the next before finally landing on *him.* My heart drops into my stomach as I take him in. Darker hair than before. It's maybe a bit longer, but not by much. When he turns his head slightly, I get a glimpse of the scruff along his jawline. It's sexy. He's sexy. But when he smiles at the bartender and the small dip in his cheek makes an appearance, I lose my mind. Well, not really, but it does trigger the few memories I have of him…of us.

I tuck a strand of hair behind my ear, straighten my sweater, and then maneuver my way through the tables toward the bar. Just like last year, there's no one here other than me, him, and the bartender. After all, it's only ten o'clock in the morning on New Year's Day, and most people are probably at home, spending time with family.

I sidle up to the stool next to him and rest my arms on the bar top.

"What can I get you?" The gruff sound of the bartender reminds me that he's not one to let you sit at his bar if you're not drinking.

I glance over at my neighbor before my eyes flit to the counter in front of him. There are no shots of magic whiskey. No rows of empty shot glasses. Only a lone glass of water. "I'll have what he's having." I motion toward my dimpled friend, and the bartender grunts.

"We charge for water," the grumpy guy says.

"Yeah, okay. I've got money." I smile and he grimaces, but that's okay. I can deal with his irritable attitude today because *he's* here.

"You're really here?" I whisper as the bartender slides my glass of water in front of me. I toss some money on the counter, mostly to get rid of him. And it works. He grabs the money before walking toward the back of the bar.

"You really left?" Bennett takes a drink of water before looking at me. His eyes narrow and he presses his lips together, forming a flat line.

"You were gone. There was no note. Nothing. Only my phone on the pillow next to me." I shift my weight until I'm facing him. "I even texted you and you never responded, so I assumed you weren't coming back, at least not as long as I was there."

Bennett shakes his head and then smiles. "Evie. Evie. Evie." He chants my name as he slides off his stool. "I live there. It's my home. Why would you even think I wouldn't be back?"

I shrug. My heart sinks a little deeper into my chest. "I guess I just thought you wanted me to leave." I drop my focus toward the floor for a beat before bringing my gaze back to his.

"Why would I want you to leave?" He takes a step toward me before reaching for my hands.

"I don't know. I mean you never replied to my text. You always reply, even when you're working." I hate to keep thinking about my ex every time something goes wrong between me and Bennett, but I can't help myself. Kyle would sometimes leave for days before coming back home to the apartment we shared together. Until the last time. He never came back, and I'm so thankful that he didn't.

"I woke up early. You looked so peaceful and beautiful lying in my bed, so I decided not to wake you. I took a shower, got dressed, and then headed out to get coffee for us. When I opened the door to my truck, I saw your phone on the console, so I brought it back in and left it on the pillow beside you." He leans in and presses his lips to mine. The kiss is soft and sweet and too short.

"Why didn't you leave a note?" I hate to let my insecurities show, but I can't help it. I need to know what he was thinking.

"I didn't leave a note because I only planned on being gone for about ten minutes, but then Mom called and asked me to run by the grocery store to pick up a few things since I was out, so that added some time. What really held me up was that I got caught in traffic. Road construction on New Year's Day—go figure." He grins. "As for the missed text, you know how bad the service is in that part of town, so for some reason, I didn't get it until about five minutes ago."

"How did you know I'd be here?" I squeeze his hands gently.

"We had a date, remember?" He wraps his strong arms around me and pulls me in close to him. My body immediately melts into his. This is what I want, what I need. So why am I so afraid of having it?

"Yeah, but—"

"There's no but to it. I promised you a date, and that's what you're gonna get. I just didn't realize we'd meet up here first. I figured I'd come home and find you still in my bed."

"Yeah, I guess I got spooked. I thought I was done with the trust issues I have, but apparently I'm not."

Bennett kisses the top of my head before pulling back and looking at me. "I'll earn your trust, Evie. I promise. And you'll see that not all guys are assholes—especially the ones who really love you."

My heart skips a beat. *Especially the ones who really love you.*

"So what are you saying?" I swallow hard and then tilt my head back slightly so I can focus on his face.

"I love you, Evie Tucker. I don't know how or why or when it happened, but over the course of a year, you've shown up at the times when I needed you most. That first night at the bar. My short stint in the hospital. The day at the cleaners, and then finally at Brock and Jade's wedding." He covers my mouth with his and kisses me long and hard before pulling away and looking into my eyes. "But I really think I fell for you over the past few months when we spent so much time talking and texting. I feel like I've known you forever." He tucks a strand of hair behind my ear and kisses my cheek.

"Me too. You make me happy, Bennett. So happy. I want this. I want us and I'm willing to let go of my insecurities and try to trust again."

I lick my lips then blow out a deep breath. I know I'm not finished. He needs to know how I feel. I press my cheek to his chest, wrap my arms around his waist, and squeeze. He holds me close to him for several minutes before I pull away. My eyes flit to his and he smiles.

"I love you too…so much that it scares me." Heat rushes to my face with my admission, but I'm being honest, and if I expect him to be trustworthy then I need to be honest about my feelings.

"Hey, Evie, I'm scared too—of so many things, but falling in love with you isn't one of them. We've got this. I promise."

I look around this shitty little bar and know deep down inside my soul that The Red Door gave me my life back. I'm not sure if was the shots of whiskey or fate, but somehow, I found this amazing guy who's not afraid to take a chance on love.

Five years later
Bennett

"DADDY, when will my momma be home?" Liam screams. I swear this kid has only one volume and it's loud.

"Aunt Tess just called and said they're on their way home now." I scoop my little screamer up in my arms and ruffle his red hair before kissing the top of his head. "Love you, buddy."

"Are they bringing my baby sister too?" He's still screaming, only now he's in my face.

"Yep. Hannah will be with them."

"Promise?" His chubby cheeks flush and his mouth forms a perfect smile.

"Yeah, buddy, I promise. Aunt Tess picked both of them up from the hospital and will deliver them safely to our house," I reassure him.

I know I should be the one at the hospital bringing my family home, but Evie insisted I stay with Liam and let Tess bring her home. She didn't like us being away from Liam so much over the past few days with the birth of Hannah. I wasn't about to argue with her, so I gave in and agreed to stay with him even though I wanted to be the one to bring her and our daughter home from the hospital.

"I wuv you, Daddy." Liam gives me a wet kiss on the cheek before fighting to get out of my arms. I set him on the floor, and he runs toward his bedroom. He has entirely too much energy.

Evie and I didn't waste any time starting our family. Liam was born on New Year's Eve the year after our second meeting at The Red Door. Then we got married on January first a year later. I love my little family, but some days I live in fear that the cancer will return and take me away from my amazing life. Still, Evie's always there to reassure me that together we can fight anything this shitty world throws at us. Plus, I'm over five years cancer-free, and that gives me hope that I've already seen my worst days.

The front door rattles, pulling my attention away from my thoughts and to my beautiful wife walking over the threshold with my daughter in her arms. My sister follows close behind with the baby carrier and a couple of bags.

Tess drops everything to the floor and looks over at me.

"You did real good with this one, baby brother." She smiles. "She hasn't let out a peep since we left the hospital. I think she may actually be a sleeper and not a screamer like—"

"Momma! Momma! You home with her." He points toward his sister.

"As I was saying, like Liam." She laughs and rushes to my boy, grabbing him up from the floor and peppering kisses all over his face.

"Stop it! Stop it!" he hollers. "I need my momma and my baby sister." He pulls away from Tess and runs toward Evie, who's now sitting on the couch with Hannah.

"Careful, little man. She's little. You have to be sweet and love on your sister gently," Evie says as she pulls the blanket away from my daughter's face. Liam moves very slowly until his lips meet her forehead. "You're such a good big brother," she tells him, and he smiles proudly.

Liam looks at me, still wearing his smile that looks so much like his mother's. "I'm a good brudder, Daddy." He's still yelling. We've really got to work on his volume control.

"I'm heading out. If you guys need anything, just call," Tess says as she walks out the front door.

"Will do. Thanks for bringing my girls home." As soon as the door shuts behind my sister, I focus my attention back on my family.

Evie is whispering something to Liam, and he covers his mouth with his finger before kissing his sister's forehead again.

"Do you want me to take her so you can get some rest?" I ask Evie, interrupting her conversation with our son. She's pale and looks tired, but she's still beautiful. Always beautiful.

She shakes her head. "No, I missed this little guy and you. I need this. I need you guys." She motions for me to sit with them.

I walk over to the couch and sit down on the opposite side of my wife.

She rests her head on my shoulder. "I love you, Bennett," she whispers softly.

I lean over slightly and brush my lips over hers. "I love you too, Evie. Thank you for giving me this life."

Her eyes flit to mine. "I didn't give you this life. We made this life together, and I'm so thankful for it."

I'm happy, healthy, and thankful, but most of all my heart is full, and my entire reason for living is piled up on this couch next to me.

The End

A NOTE FROM THE AUTHOR

Dear Reader,

I hope you enjoyed reading Evie and Bennett's story as much as I enjoyed writing it. These two found happiness during a time when day to day life was a struggle. Thank you for being a part of Evie and Bennett's journey to finding their happily ever after.

Cheers,
Emery xoxo

About the Author

Emery grew up in Southern Arkansas and has lived most of her adult life in Northern Louisiana. She spends her days working as a Nurse Practitioner in rural health and her nights reading, writing, and occasionally sleeping.

She loves real life romance…lots of angst and heartbreak, but always a happy ending.

To learn more visit her website.

Sign up for Emery's newsletter and receive the latest news and updates on her books, releases, and sales.

Join her reader's group.

Twisted Fate Series:

Twisted Fate

Twisted Surprise (A Twisted Fate Christmas Novella)

Beautiful Tomorrow

Velvet Thunder Series:

Everything That Glitters

Standalones:

Undeniably His

My Blue

Acknowledgments

There are so many people to thank for being a part of this book writing journey. It would've been impossible to do alone.

Taylor Roth—Thank you for being the BEST PA ever!! Without you none of the important stuff would ever get done. Many—Many—thanks for designing graphics (teasers, FB Banners, etc.), making sign up forms that somehow become organized spreadsheets, BETA reading and telling me the TRUTH, promoting everything I write, hanging out with me and the BABES, listening to me talk about absolutely nothing for longer than you probably want to, and for organizing EVERYTHING. I'm sure I left some stuff out, but I hope you know how much I appreciate you!!

Claudia Burgoa—Thank you for all your help. You are a true friend and I appreciate you more than you can imagine.

Dawn with Evident Ink: I couldn't ask for a better developmental editor. Thank you so much for your guidance and direction. Without you I'd never finish writing anything.

Caitlin with C. Marie Editing: Thank you for cleaning

up my manuscript and making my words sound pretty. Thank you for always doing an excellent job.

Julie Deaton: Thank you for being my final set of eyes for this project. And thank you for always loving my stories.

Debra and Drue with Buoni Amici Press PR—Thank you for keeping me organized. Thanks for going above and beyond to promote my books and keep my social media sites up and running. I'm very thankful for both of you.

Taylor and Rachael—my betas. You guys are fabulous! Thank you for your honesty and ability to always guide me in the right direction.

To my husband—you are wonderful, but I guess you already knew that, huh? Thanks for putting up with my many hours locked away in my office or talking about this book to the point of making you want to go anywhere just to get away from the sound of my voice.

To my son—Thank you for being you. My absolute greatest accomplishment. I'm thankful every day that I'm your mom.

To my mom: Thank you for always believing in me and giving me the freedom to make my own decisions. Sometimes it took me the long way around to get to where I was supposed to be, but I always made it.

To my Dad—I miss you every day. You always supported me and believed in me. Thank you for being the best Dad ever!

Taylor with Southern Side Designs: Thank you for designing the perfect cover for The Red Door. It is beautiful!

Wander Aguiar: Thank you for the perfect image for the cover of The Red Door. And thank you for always being so kind and easy to work with.

To every blogger, reader, author, and friend who has shared my teasers and cover, or who has promoted my book —thank you—because without your support no one would know my books existed.

Emery Jacobs' Book Babes—Thank you for supporting me and waiting patiently for me to release books. You guys are the VERY BEST!!

To the readers—thank you for taking a chance on a new author. You guys are amazing! I really hope you loved Evie and Bennett's story as much as I loved writing it.

www.ingramcontent.com/pod-product-compliance
Lightning Source LLC
Chambersburg PA
CBHW021232130726
47988CB00002B/936